a b c d e f

g h i j k l

m n o p q r

s t u v w x

y z

A B C D E F

G H I J K L

M N O P Q R

S T U V W X

Y Z

CUENTO
DE LUZ

To the Ayobamis, who represent all the children in the world who wish to go to school.
— Pilar López Ávila —

To my family: Thank you for always being by my side.
— Mar Azabal —

Waterproof and tear resistant
Produced without water, without trees and without bleach
Saves 50% of energy compared to normal paper

Ayobami and the Names of the Animals
Text © 2017 Pilar López Ávila
Illustrations © 2017 Mar Azabal
This edition © 2017 Cuento de Luz SL
Calle Claveles, 10 | Urb. Monteclaro | Pozuelo de Alarcón | 28223 | Madrid | Spain
www.cuentodeluz.com
Title in Spanish: Ayobami y el nombre de los animales
English translation by Jon Brokenbrow
Second printing
Printed in PRC by Shanghai Chenxi Printing Co., Ltd. March 2018, print number 1631-1
ISBN: 978-84-16733-42-2

AYOBAMI
AND THE NAMES OF THE ANIMALS

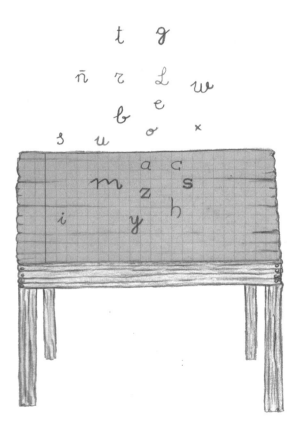

Pilar López Ávila
Mar Azabal

When the war finally came to an end, the teacher went from house to house, telling everyone that the children could go back to school the next day.

The children ran out into the street, shouting with joy.
They laughed and they hugged each other.
They were very, very happy.

As the sun rose, Ayobami got up and dressed, before her father came in to wake her up.

He gave her a piece of paper, and a worn-out pencil.

"Wait for the other kids, so you don't have to go on your own," he said.

But she was so impatient to get back to school, she didn't want to wait for anyone.

"I really want to learn to read and write!"

So her father made her a little boat, out of another piece of paper.

He pushed it out onto the river that ran past their home, and said:

"Follow it downstream, and you'll arrive at the schoolhouse."

Ayobami followed the little paper boat as it sailed down the river, until it got stuck on a branch.

It stayed there for a little while, until it finally sank.

Ayobami felt sad as she watched it. How was she going to get to school now?

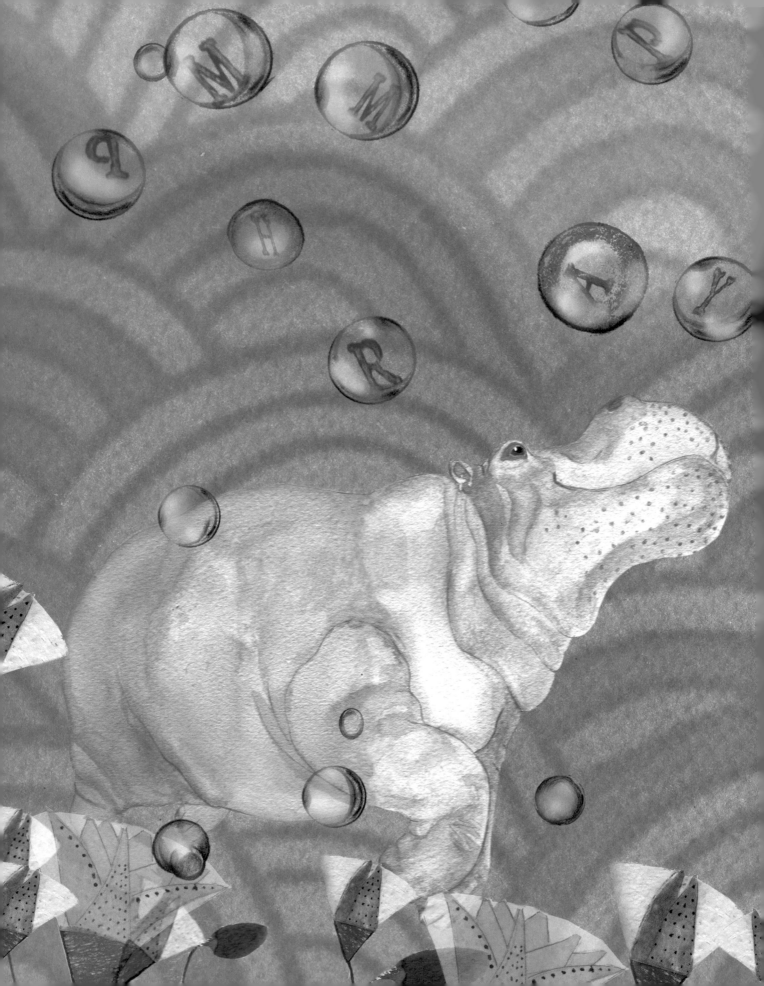

A hippopotamus was watching her from the river bank.

"What's wrong, little girl?" he said.

Ayobami told him that her paper boat had sunk, and now she didn't know how to get to school.

"Well, I can show you the quickest way, but you have to promise me that when you come back, you'll write my name for me!"

The little girl nodded her head.

"The quickest, but most dangerous way, is through the jungle. There are lots of animals there that will want to eat you up, but if you don't stop, you'll reach the schoolhouse."

So Ayobami took the path that led through the jungle.

As she was walking along the path, a crocodile that had been hiding in the bushes jumped out in front of her.

"Where are you going, little girl?" he asked.

"I'm going to school, to learn to read and write," she said.

"Now why would you want to read and write?" asked the crocodile.

"So that … so that I can write your name. Let me go on my way, and when I come back from school, I'll write it down on a piece of paper."

"Very well," said the crocodile. "I'll be waiting for you here. Off you go."

The crocodile moved out of the way, and Ayobami kept walking, without looking back.

A leopard that had been resting on a branch jumped down in front of her.

"Where are you going, little girl?" he asked.

"I'm going to school, because I want to learn to read and write. If you don't eat me, when I come back I'll write your name on a piece of paper."

The leopard looked at her, thinking about what Ayobami had said.

"Very well. I hope you do it."

And he moved out of her way.

S S S S S S

Then, a long, green snake slithered across the path.

"Hello, little girl. I'm very hungry, and it's breakfast time," she hissed.

"Don't eat me! When I come back from school, I'll write your name on a piece of paper!" said Ayobami.

"Hmmm … I've never seen my name written on a piece of paper before."

And she moved out of the way, so Ayobami could keep walking.

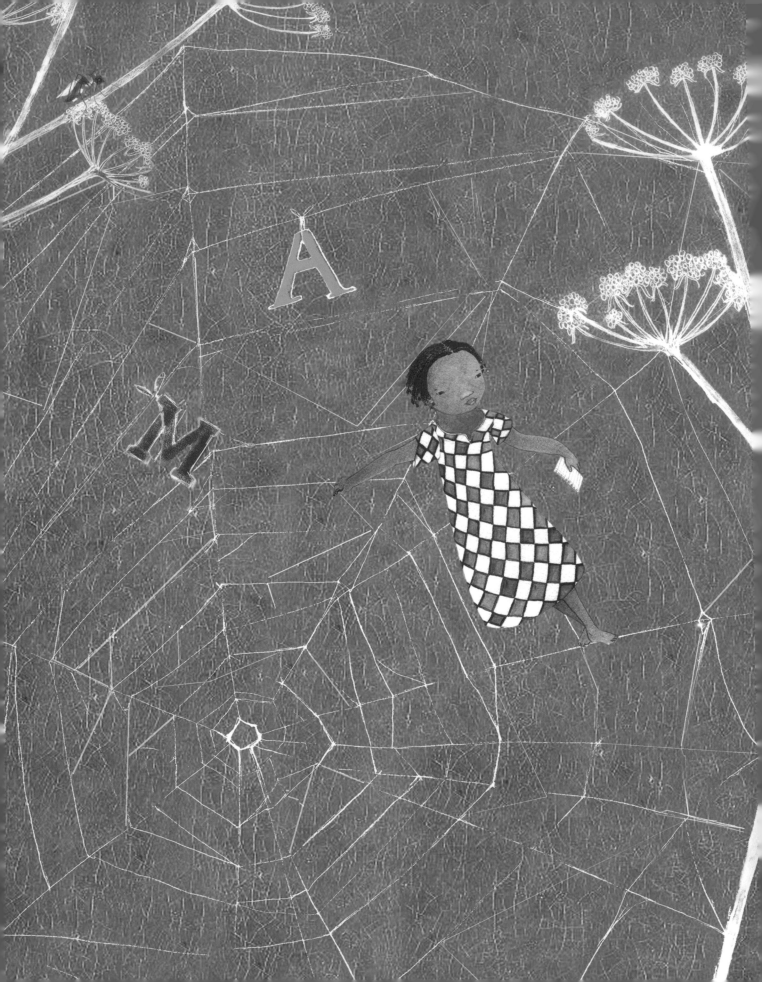

Next, a big, hairy spider with long legs jumped out in front of her.

"I've never had a little girl for breakfast," said the spider.

But Ayobami told the spider that she would write her name, if the spider let her pass.

The spider agreed, and Ayobami kept on walking.

Then a tiny mosquito buzzed in front of her.

"Even though you can hardly see me, I'm more dangerous than you think," said the mosquito.

Ayobami begged her to let her keep walking to school, and in exchange she would write her name on a piece of paper.

The mosquito agreed, and told Ayobami that she would be waiting in the same place when she came back.

Ayobami finally crossed through the jungle, and was the first to arrive at the schoolhouse. The teacher was waiting by the door.

The other children, who had taken the path that ran alongside the river, soon arrived.

In class, Ayobami learned the letters of the alphabet.

She learned how to put them together to make sounds.

To join the sounds to make words.

To mix the words together to make sentences.

And she heard the music that comes from making words.

When school was over, Ayobami said goodbye to her teacher.

In her hand, she had a piece of paper, with writing on only one side. And she set off along the path through the jungle.

mosquito

spider

snake

The MOSQUITO was waiting.

She gave it the piece of paper with its name, and the insect flew off, happily.

The SPIDER was also waiting.

It took the piece of paper with its name, waving its hairy legs in the air.

The SNAKE was twisted around a branch.

It slid down to the ground, and disappeared into the trees, with the piece of paper with its name.

The LEOPARD jumped out of the tree when it saw Ayobami walking by.

It climbed back up with the piece of paper, and fell back to sleep.

The CROCODILE appeared out of the shadows.

It read the piece of paper with its name, and walked off with a big smile on its face.

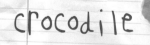

crocodile

hippopotamus

leopard

Ayobami walked out of the jungle, and gave the
HIPPOPOTAMUS the last piece of paper she had left.

And it sank back down to the bottom of the river with it
in its mouth.

The sun began to set, and Ayobami's parents sat by the door, waiting for her to come home.

"Show me what you have learned," said her father.

But Ayobami didn't have any paper left, and the pencil was all worn out.

Her father walked back into the house with an angry expression, believing that his daughter had wasted her time at school.

Her mother gave her a big hug.

Ayobami sat by the door, waiting for night to fall.

In the middle of the night, a very strong wind began to blow.

It was so strong that it blew the dust from the paths.

It churned up the water in the river.

It blew all of the fallen leaves from the floor of the jungle.

It woke up all of the animals, who were dreaming about their names, written on a piece of paper.

Just before Ayobami woke up, the wind blew against the door of her house. Her father opened the door, and found a piece of paper with writing on it. It was made of little scraps of paper, all joined together. Each one had a word on it.

Ayobami climbed out of bed, and read out the words:

MOSQUITO, SPIDER, SNAKE, LEOPARD, CROCODILE, HIPPOPOTAMUS

Ayobami's father understood that she had learned to read and write at school. He understood that she had made the animals dream about the sound of their names.

Clutching another piece of paper and another little stub of a pencil, the little girl set off to school again, along the path that leads to the place where hope is born.

A B C D E F
G H I J K L
M N O P Q R
S T U V W X
Y Z

a b c d e f
g h i j k l
m n o p q r
s t u v w x
y z

a   b   c   d   e   f

g   h   i   j   k   l

m   n   o   p   q   r

s   t   u   v   w   x

y   z

A   B   C   D   E   F

G   H   I   J   K   L

M   N   O   P   Q   R

S   T   U   V   W   X

Y   Z

Ayobami

A B C D E F

G H I J K L

M N O P Q R

S T U V W X

Y Z

a b c d e f

g h i j k l

m n o p q r

s t u v w x

y z